THIS BOOK BELONGS TO

....

....

HEY DUGGEE

LADYBIRD BOOKS

UK | USA | Canada | Ireland | Australia | India | New Zealand | South Africa

Ladybird Books is part of the Penguin Random House group of companies whose addresses can be found at global.penguinrandomhouse.com.

www.penguin.co.uk   www.puffin.co.uk   www.ladybird.co.uk

Penguin Random House UK

First published 2022
001

Text and illustrations copyright © Studio AKA Limited, 2022
Adapted by Rebecca Gerlings

Printed in China
The authorized representative in the EEA is Penguin Random House Ireland,
Morrison Chambers, 32 Nassau Street, Dublin DO2 YH68

A CIP catalogue record for this book is available from the British Library

ISBN: 978-1-40595-079-4

All correspondence to:
Ladybird Books
Penguin Random House Children's
One Embassy Gardens, 8 Viaduct Gardens, London SW11 7BW

THE SPACE BADGE

DUGGEE

ROLY

NORRIE

BETTY

HAPPY

TAG

It's snowy, and the Squirrels are bored. They stare out of the clubhouse window and sigh.
"It's too dark to play outside," says Tag.

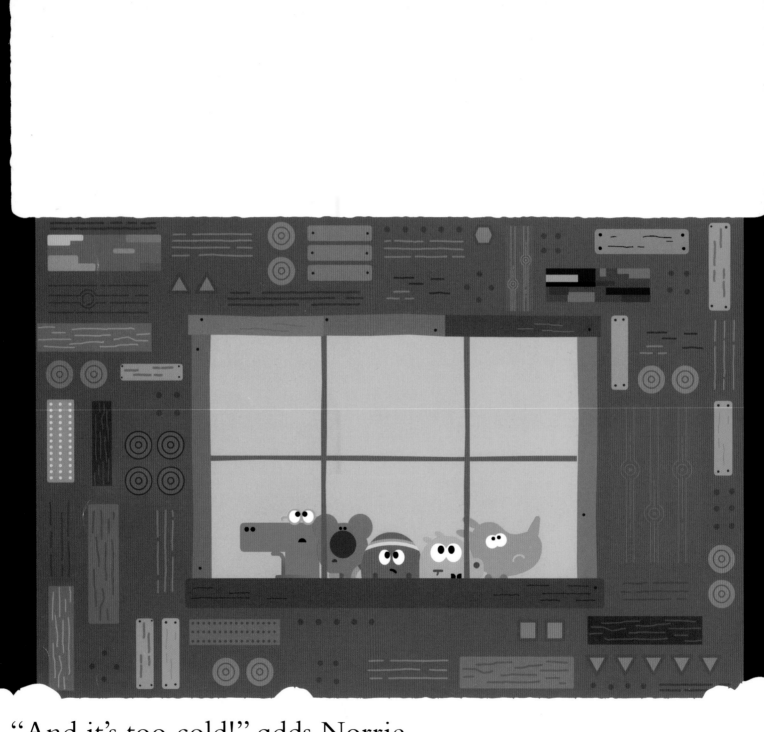

"And it's too cold!" adds Norrie.

Maybe Duggee can help?
"Hey, Duggee. What are you doing?"
ask the Squirrels.
"Ah-woof!" Duggee's looking at the
solar system through a telescope.

"What's the solar system?" asks Betty. Duggee can explain. He has his **Space Badge!**

The Squirrels will pretend to be the planets –
and Duggee will be the sun!

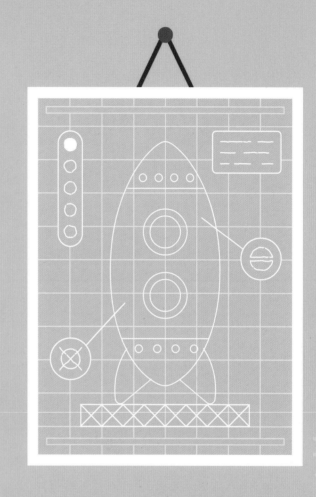

"The *sun*?" asks Tag.
That's right. The sun.

The sun is a star, burning brightly at
the centre of our solar system.
"WOW!" gasp the Squirrels.

Roly is Mercury.

Happy is Venus.

Norrie is Earth.

Tag is Mars.

Betty is Jupiter.

That just
leaves . . .

Saturn . . .

BUCAW!

Uranus . . .

BOING!

and Neptune!

POP!

And here are all the planets together, spinning round the sun. This is our solar system.

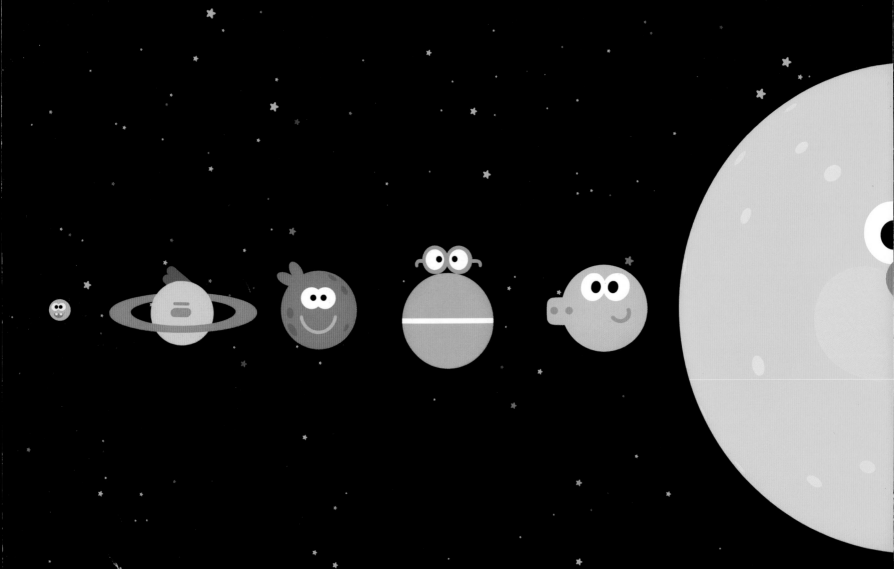

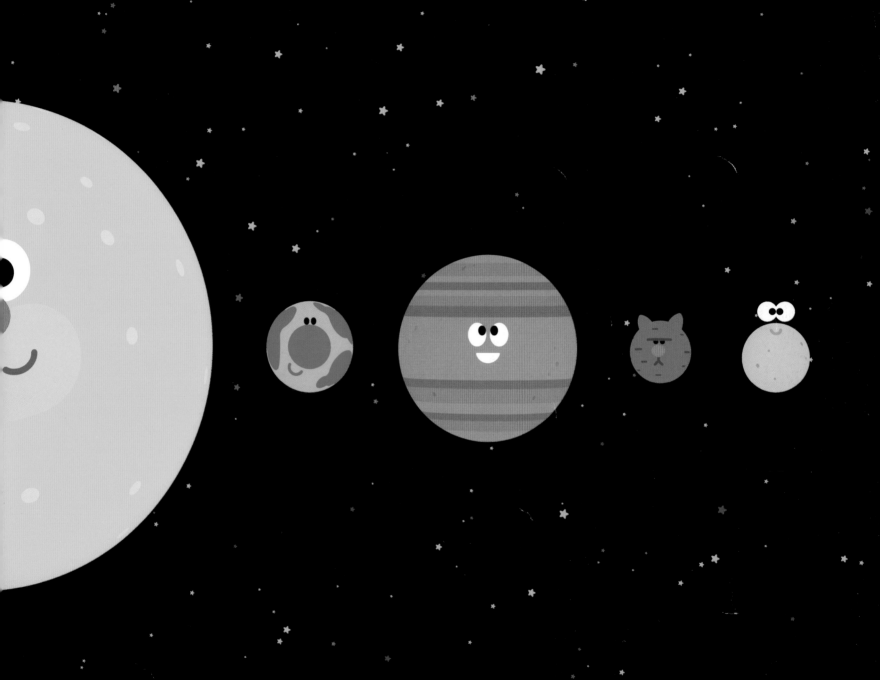

"AMAZING!" cry the Squirrels.
"I wish I could go into space!" says Betty.

That would be fun. But all these planets are millions of miles away! You'd need a rocket ship to travel into space . . .

Duggee's got one of those!

5, 4, 3, 2, 1...

They zoom towards the stars in Duggee's rocket ship.

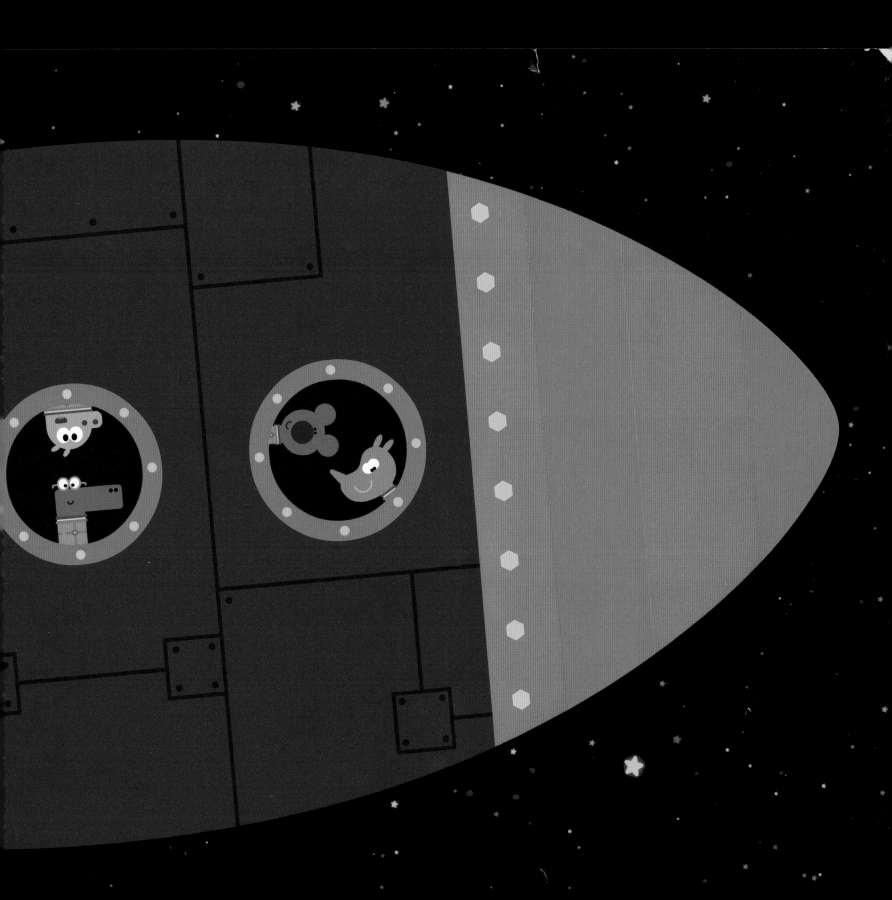

What will the Squirrels find out here?

Duggee and the Squirrels zip along
towards Jupiter and Saturn.
"So much space . . ." says Happy.
"For playing!" adds Tag.

"Where's the space playground, Duggee?" asks Norrie.
Sadly, there are no playgrounds in space.

OR PADDLING POOLS.

OR BOUNCY CASTLES.

OR TREEHOUSES.

OR TOILETS!

But there are *lots* of other things. AMAZING things, like . . .

. . . the Milky Way . . .

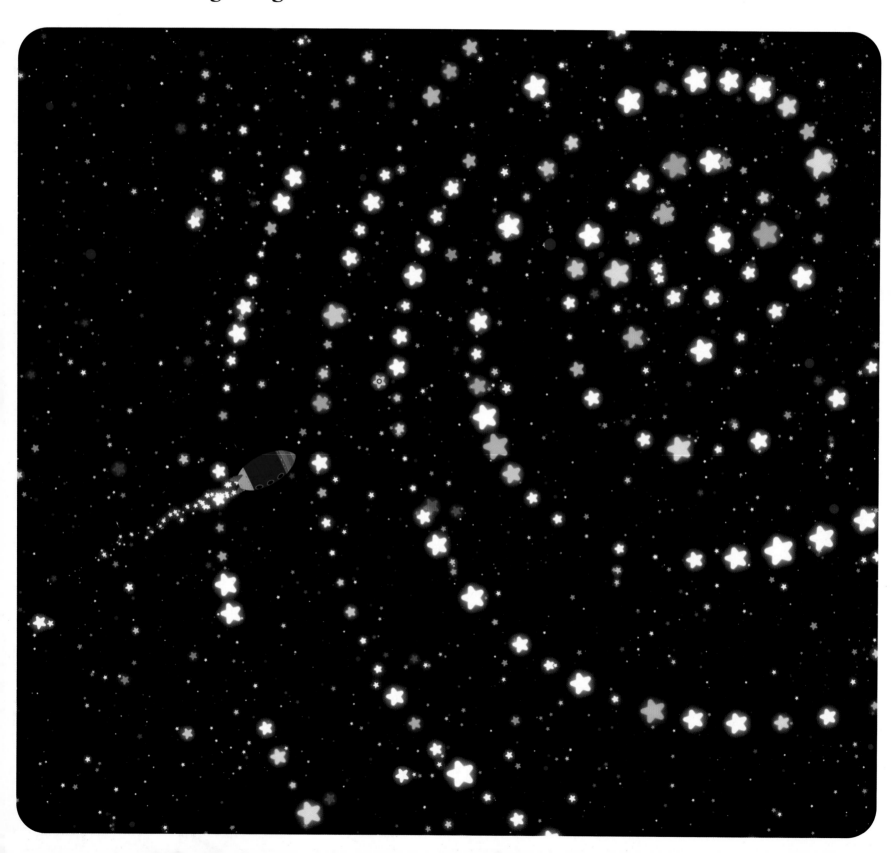

the asteroid belt . . .

and cosmic comets!

"Are we going home now?" asks Happy.
"Ah-woof!" replies Duggee.
"But we haven't seen anyone yet!" cries Betty.
"What about *aliens*?" asks Tag.

Little green ones . . . big purple ones . . . really weird ones . . .

cute little ones . . . even invisible ones!

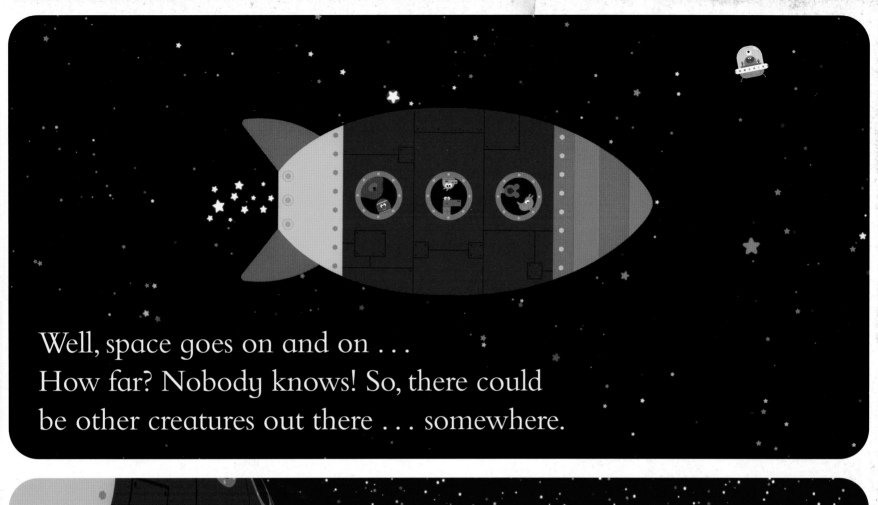

Well, space goes on and on ...
How far? Nobody knows! So, there could
be other creatures out there ... somewhere.

But now it's time to head back to Earth ...

Haven't the Squirrels done well today, Duggee?

AH-WOOF!

They have definitely earned their **Space Badges**.

Now there's just time for one last
thing before the Squirrels go home . . .

"DUGGEE HUG!"